It's Christmas Again!

By
**Frrich Lewandowski &
Michael P. Riccards**

Illustrations by
Kathryn H. Delisle

Ambassador Books • Worcester, Massachusetts

ISBN: 1-929039-04-2
Library of Congress Catalog Card Number: 00-105705

Published in the United States by Ambassador Books, Inc.
71 Elm Street, Worcester, Massachusetts 01609
(800) 577-0909

Printed in Hong Kong.

For current information about all titles from Ambassador Books, visit our website at:
www.ambassadorbooks.com

*Dedicated to children everywhere
whose innocence and wonder
remind us of the
deeper and fuller meaning of
Jesus' presence in our world.*

Other books by
Frrich Lewandowski:

Babci's Angel

The First Easter Bunny

Shooting Stardust

I t snowed all day. After school, the children made snowmen and built snow forts in the playground. Then, Michael and his brother, Matthew, went to Jeffrey's house. Mrs. Anderson, Jeffrey's mother, gave them hot chocolate and homemade cookies.

Michael asked, "How many days until December 25th?"

"Only 10 more days," Mrs. Anderson replied.

December 25th was everyone's favorite day! For weeks before the big day, people rushed from store to store buying toys and other gifts. They strung bright lights on the outside of their homes. And in their living rooms, they decorated real trees with shining bulbs and strings of silver called "tinsel."

Then, on the morning of December 25th, when children awoke, they found presents under the tree—gifts from a man named "Santa."

"Mom, why does Santa bring us gifts on December 25th?" Jeffrey asked.

"Because he likes you, I guess," Mrs. Anderson replied.

"But why on December 25th?" Michael continued.

"It's a tradition," she answered.

"What's a *tradition*?" Michael asked.

"It's just the way something has always been done."

"I still don't understand," Jeffrey's sister, Emily, said. "Why has Santa always brought gifts?"

Mrs. Anderson was puzzled. "I don't know," she said. "Why don't you ask Mr. Greene tomorrow. I'm sure he'll know."

Before supper, Jeffrey did his homework, but he kept thinking about December 25th.

"Why?" he wondered. "Why?"

"Mom, why do we put a tree in our house before December 25th?" he asked.

"It's just a tradition, like getting gifts from Santa. Maybe you could ask Mr. Greene about that, too," his mother replied.

At supper, Jeffrey kept
asking questions about
December 25th. His parents
could not answer his questions.
This made him wonder even
more.

When Jeffrey saw his teacher Mr. Greene the next day, he ran up to him and exclaimed, "Mr. Greene, you must know why people celebrate December 25th!"

Mr. Greene thought for a moment.

"It's just a tradition," he said.

"But *why* is it a tradition?" asked Jeffrey.

"I really don't know. I'll ask my grandmother," Mr. Greene said. "She's quite old, maybe she will remember."

That evening, Mr. Greene visited his grandmother.

"There definitely is a reason for celebrating December 25th," Grandmother Greene said.

"When I was a little girl, adults told a story about the holiday. But it was so many years ago, I can't remember what they said."

"I don't have an answer for you," Mr. Greene told his class the next day.

"Nobody—not even my grandmother—knows why we celebrate December 25th. But I would like to know. And you would like to know, too. So for your homework assignment, find out why we celebrate December 25th."

As the days passed, the children asked everyone they knew about December 25th. But no one could tell them why people celebrate that day.

14

Finally, December 25th arrived! There were so many new toys that the children were too excited to care about the reason for the holiday. They just wanted to play with their new toys.

That afternoon, Jeffrey and his sisters went outside to play with Michael and Matthew.

They passed a neighbor's barn and decided to go in and pet the animals. They often went to the barn to see the animals. But this time, something was different. As they neared the barn door, they heard voices. They entered the barn very quietly to see who was talking.

What they saw amazed them.

An owl sat high on a rafter talking "people talk." The other animals sat very quietly and listened as the owl told a story.

"Many years ago, a man names Joseph and his wife, Mary, were on a long trip. Mary was about to have a baby. So Joseph tried to find a place for them to stay. There was no room for them anywhere. So Mary and Joseph stayed in a cave with animals like us.

"One very dark night, Mary gave birth to a baby boy. Because this baby was special, Mary gave him the name *Jesus*."

"What made him so special?" asked the goat.

17

"He is the Son of God," the owl said.

"When he was born, angels came down from heaven and sang beautiful songs. And a bright star appeared in the sky over the cave.

"Shepherds came to see the baby Jesus. They knelt down and worshiped him.

"And I bet that at night, the lambs cuddled close to the family to keep them warm," the owl said proudly.

"Then, three wise men came from a distant land. They had followed the bright star to the cave.

"They, too, knelt and worshiped the baby. They said he was a new-born king. They brought him expensive gifts—gold, frankincense, and sweet-smelling oil called myrrh."

The owl stared at the other animals.

"The birth of this baby was *the* most important event that ever took place on Earth. The animals in the cave were the first to see God's baby Son, Jesus."

"People have forgotten about Jesus, but we animals must never forget!" the owl insisted. "Instead, we must tell the story every year on December 25th, so the birth of Jesus will never be forgotten!"

20

Then the owl turned to the goose.

"Go to the corner of the barn and flap your wings near the pile of hay," the owl ordered.

The goose raised her mighty wings and flapped. At first, nothing happened. So the goose moved closer to the pile of hay. She flapped her wings again. Suddenly, hay flew everywhere and a little manger appeared where the pile of hay had been. In the manger, were small statues of Joseph, Mary, the baby Jesus, and some animals.

"Many years ago, some people stored this manger here. Every year at this time, the people would come and take the manger to their home and place it under a lovely decorated tree," the owl said.

"Then they stopped coming. They forgot about the Baby's birthday. Their children forgot, too. Now everyone has forgotten Jesus' birthday. Only the animals remember. And *we* must never forget!"

"Wow!" cried Emily.

"Who's there?" asked the donkey.

"Sssh!" said the goose.

"Be quiet both of you," hushed the cow, who then began to "mooo."

Then the sheep "baa-ed" and the cat "meowed."

"We heard you talking "people talk", " said Matthew.

"Hoooo!" cried the owl, high upon his perch.

"You," pointed Allison.

"No, he didn't," protested the donkey.

Jeffrey laughed. "There you go again. You're talking "people talk" now!"

23

"So you know we can talk "people talk." So what?" said the owl.

"What you don't know is that today is Jesus' birthday!

"People have been so busy with gifts and trees and colored lights, they have forgotten what December 25th is all about.

"They have forgotten that on this day, the Son of God was born."

"May we come a little closer?" asked Jeffrey.

The goose waved them toward the manger and said,

"Of course, you may."

25

The children
knelt before the manger
to get a closer look.

A deep silence fell on
the children and the ani-
mals.

Then, the birds began to sing:

"Silent night . . . holy night.
  All is calm . . . all is bright."

Soon the others joined in:

" 'Round yon Virgin, Mother and Child.
  Holy Infant so tender and mild . . .
  Sleep in heavenly peace . . . sleep in heavenly peace."

When they finished singing, the children and the animals were filled with joy.

"Let's go tell our parents and Mr. Greene about what we have found," Michael said.

"I don't think they'll believe us," Matthew replied.

Just then, a dog ran into the barn.

"Come out quickly," the dog barked.

The children and the animals rushed outside. A bright star was shining above the barn.

They were so amazed that at first they did not notice all the people who had rushed to the barn. Michael and Matthew's parents were there, and so were Jeffrey, Allison, and Emily's parents. In fact, it looked like the whole town had come to the barn.

"It's Jesus' birthday! It's Jesus' birthday!" the children shouted. "He's the Son of God!"

The children brought everyone into the barn and led them to the manger. Mr. Greene and his grandmother made their way though the crowd. Grandmother Greene looked at the manger, and she began to cry.

"I remember now," she said, and in a hushed voice she told the story of the birth of Jesus.

When Grandmother Greene finished her story, they heard beautiful music in the distance.

As they listened, the music grew louder and louder:

"O come, let us adore Him . . .
O come, let us adore Him . . .
O come, let us adore Him . . .
Christ, the Lord."

The animals joined in singing:

"O come all ye faithful,
Joyful and triumphant
O come ye, o come ye to Bethlehem.
Come and behold Him,
Born the King of Angels . . ."

31

and the people joined in:

"O come, let us adore Him . . .
O come, let us adore Him . . .
O come, let us adore Him . . .
Christ, the Lord."

And for the children and the adults, and even for the animals, December 25th had become **Christmas Again!**